To Kelly Sonnack, for all
the doors you've opened for me
—AH

Dedicated to my grandfather, "Gunya," who
would've enjoyed researching Georgian town houses
as much as I did and chuckled at roguish Mr. Fox
—AC

 little bee books

An imprint of Bonnier Publishing USA
251 Park Avenue South, New York, NY 10010
Text copyright © 2018 by Alastair Heim
Illustrations copyright © 2018 by Alisa Coburn
LITTLE BEE BOOKS is a trademark of Bonnier Publishing USA, and associated colophon
is a trademark of Bonnier Publishing USA.
Manufactured in China   HH 0917
First Edition   10 9 8 7 6 5 4 3 2 1
ISBN 978-1-4998-0536-9
Library of Congress Cataloging-in-Publication Data
Names: Heim, Alastair, author. | Coburn, Alisa, illustrator.
Title: Hello, door / by Alastair Heim; illustrated by Alisa Coburn.
Description: First edition. | New York, NY: Little Bee Books, [2018]
Summary: Illustrations and simple, rhyming text follow a fox as he enters a home
and walks through, greeting and taking various objects, until the owners return.
Identifiers: LCCN 2017003447 | Subjects: | CYAC: Stories in rhyme. | Robbers and
outlaws—Fiction. | Foxes—Fiction. | Bears—Fiction. | Humorous stories.
Classification: LCC PZ8.3.H41336 Hel 2018 | DDC [E]—dc23
LC record available at https://lccn.loc.gov/2017003447

littlebeebooks.com
bonnierpublishingusa.com

HELLO, DOOR

by Alastair Heim   illustrated by Alisa Coburn

little bee books

Hello, door.

Hello, house.

Hello, mat.

Hello, mouse.

Hello, window.

Hello, sink.

Hello, sandwich.

Hello, drink.

Hello, sofa.   **Hello, chairs.**

Hello, mirror.

Hello, stairs.

Hello, rug.

Hello, plants.

AH-CHOO!
AH-CHOO!

Hello, Mr. Fancy Pants.

Hello, bedroom.

Hello, robes.

Hello, pretty water globes.

Hello, closet.

Hello, coat.

Hello, airplane
AND remote.

HELLO,
LITTLE JEWELRY BOX!

Hello, necklace.

Hello, rings.

Bye-bye,
bedroom.

Bye-bye, stairs.

Bye-bye, mirror.

Bye-bye . . .

...BEARS?!?

Hello, floor.

Hello, window...

Hello, door!

JAN   2018